1/2 af.

D1494758

Yours Sincerely, Giraffe

MEGUMI IWASA

Illustrations by Jun Takabatake

GECKO PRESS

Dear Reader

Tell me, how do you spend your days?

Do you have good friends? Or are you all alone?

Do you have lots and lots to do? Or are you feeling bored?

Let me introduce you to Giraffe.

"Write my story," Giraffe said. "It's perfect for people who are alone. And for people who are bored. And even people who are busy might like to take a little break and read it, too."

Contents

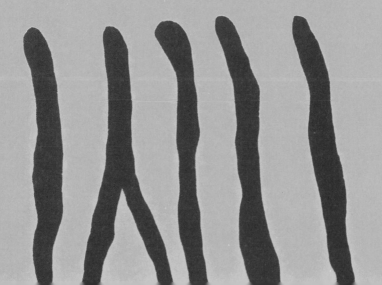

A Bored Giraffe Writes His First Letter

This is the African savanna, home to one bored giraffe.

On this day, like every other day, the sky was clear and blue. Cream puff clouds drifted slowly by, a gentle breeze crossed the plain, and there was an endless supply of acacia leaves, which Giraffe loved to eat.

Sounds perfect, you say? You're quite right.

Giraffe had everything he needed.

But, in fact, there was one thing he was missing—an extra special friend. He had no one to share his feelings with. And so, alas, he was a very bored giraffe.

And one more boring day was coming to an end.

Today was just the same as ever. Nothing happened, as usual. And I am just the same as ever. Bored, as usual.

Giraffe watched the sun slip slowly out of sight. The horizon was mirrored in his big round eyes.

Suddenly he blinked.

I wonder what's on the other side, he thought. *And what sort of animals live there?*

He stretched his long neck as far as it would go. But he couldn't see beyond the savanna.

Wait! I know. I'll write a letter!

Where did he get that idea? Well, when he was munching on leaves that afternoon, he had happened to see this sign hanging from a tree.

ANNOUNCING A NEW MAIL SERVICE
WILLING TO DELIVER ANYTHING ANYWHERE. CONTACT ME ANYTIME.
FEE: UP TO YOU
FROM: A BORED PELICAN

A bored pelican—that sounds just like me, thought Giraffe. *Maybe if I write a letter, I'll feel less bored. And if I use the new delivery service, Pelican will feel less bored, too... Yes, that's what I'll do: I'll write a letter.*

That night, Giraffe fell asleep feeling much happier than usual as he thought about all the things he wanted to say.

The next day, he wrote his very first letter and took it straight to Pelican.

Pelican was a little nervous. After all, this was his first customer. "Welcome to the Pelican Delivery Service. Where shall I take your letter?"

Giraffe was a little nervous, too. "Give it to the first animal you meet on the other side of the horizon," he said.

"The horizon? Er... You mean that place over there?" Pelican pointed to the border between the bright blue sky and the green savanna.

"That's right." Giraffe was beginning to feel excited. "And please bring back a reply."

"Of course! The horizon doesn't look very far. I should be able to make it there and back before the sun goes down."

Pelican flapped his wings and flew up in the air, higher and higher, as if he were being sucked into the sky.

"Be sure to get a reply!" Giraffe shouted.

"Okaaaaaay!"

In no time, Pelican had shrunk to a tiny little speck and disappeared.

Is the Horizon Near? Or Far?

Pelican had said he would be back before sundown, but it was now long past sunset and darkness had fallen.

Giraffe sighed. *I doubt that even Pelican can fly in the dark. I guess there's no point in staying up all night. I'd better go to bed.*

He gently closed his eyes. Even though Pelican had not returned, Giraffe still felt peaceful inside. *It's all right. I'm sure he'll come back with a letter from the other side of the horizon.*

From early the next morning, the not-so-bored Giraffe watched the sky for Pelican's return.

He craned his neck so eagerly that it grew two inches.

By the time noon rolled around, Giraffe's neck
had stretched another inch. Then, at last, there
he was! The long-awaited Pelican.

Giraffe was popping with excitement. He
could see something in Pelican's beak. "Hurry!"
he shouted. "Show me the letter. Quick! Quick!"

But Pelican gave him a long, hard look.

"Now listen here, Giraffe," he said. "Do you have any idea how hard that job was?"

Giraffe realized he was being impatient, so he took a deep breath.

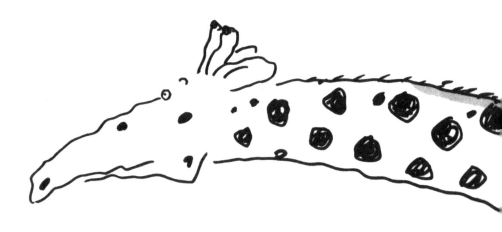

"It was that hard, was it?" he said. "Here, let me get you something to eat. Put down your bag and have a good long rest."

Oh dear, thought Giraffe as the words left his mouth. *Why on earth did I tell him to take a LONG rest?*

He was dying to read the letter that very minute.

Pelican ate until his belly was full and his heart content. Then he told Giraffe his story.

Although the horizon had looked close, it was very far away. No matter how far he flew, he never seemed to get any closer. When he finally reached the other side, all that he could see was water. There was more water than any lake he had ever seen in Africa.

"You said to give the letter to the first animal I met on the other side of the horizon, right?" Pelican said.

"That's right." Giraffe nodded.

"Well, the first animal I met was named Seal. 'Here's a letter,' I said. 'Please bring me a reply.'

'Will do!' he said, and then he zoomed away."

Pelican discovered that the big water was called Whale Sea and that Seal's job was to deliver all the mail there.

Pelican was particularly impressed to hear that Seal had just won an award for being such a hard worker.

"But then who got my letter?" Giraffe asked. He was beginning to feel a little worried.

In a very small voice, Pelican said, "Well, it seems that the only animal in Whale Sea that ever gets letters is…er…Someone-or-other."

Giraffe leaned forward eagerly. "And did you meet this Someone-or-other?"

"No, no, that's not his name. Actually, it sounded something like my name… Let me think for a moment."

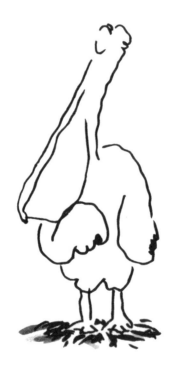

Pelican tried hard to remember the name, but
that was the last thing Giraffe cared about.
All he could think of was opening that letter.
He wasn't bored any longer. His heart was
pounding as if his whole body were a drum.

Thumpity-thump, thumpity-thump,
Boom-diddy-boom, boom-diddy-boom.

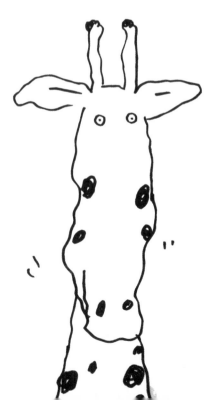

Pelican couldn't stop talking about his first delivery job. By the time he finally went home, it was already dark.

I never did find out the name of that Someone-or-other, thought Giraffe. He wanted to read the reply right now, but he would have to wait until morning. The moon was just a tiny sliver, and the night was far too dark to read.

Can you guess who got Giraffe's letter? His name sounds a little like Pelican. If you guessed Penguin, you're right.

Shall we take a peek at Penguin's life?

Penguin and the Magnificent Professor Whale

Just as Seal had said, the only animal in Whale Sea who got letters was Penguin. Most were from his girlfriend, but sometimes he got letters from his mother or father.

He had left his home on Penguin Island to live at Whale Point.

Whale Point was just a tiny bit of land that jutted out into Whale Sea.

Once, long ago, so many whales had lived in the sea that the water was black with them. Now, however, there was only one old whale left.

But he was no ordinary whale. He was Professor Whale of Whale Point School.

And Penguin was his student. There was no school on Penguin's island, so he was studying abroad.

There were two reasons that Professor Whale was a teacher: because he was extraordinarily big and because he was extraordinarily old. In other words, because he was, quite simply, extraordinary.

And he was especially good at spouting. No one could spout like him.

Everyone clapped when he sent a magnificent spout high into the air. Privately, he had decided to retire from teaching when he could no longer spout like that.

But he did not need to worry yet. His spout was still stupendous.

Penguin was the only student in the school.

On this particular day, he was studying as usual. The topic was "the mysteries of the sea."

"Describe the sea for me," said Professor Whale.

"Why, it's blue, sir," Penguin answered.

"Blue? A good start! Bring me some seawater and show me."

Penguin filled a bucket from the sea and took it to the Professor.

"Hmmm," said the Professor. "What have we here? It doesn't look blue at all."

"What? That can't be right." But when Penguin looked into the bucket, it was true. In fact, the seawater was completely transparent. "That's strange. Let me try again."

But no matter how many times he tried, the water in the bucket was never blue. He looked first at the blue water in the sea, and then at the water in the bucket, and sighed. It just didn't make sense.

At that very moment, Seal arrived. "Penguin, I have a letter for you."

Penguin thought it must be from his girlfriend, but Seal said, "No, not today. This time it's from someone new."

"Really? Who?" Penguin asked.

"Someone whose name sounds a lot like yours. No, wait a minute. That was the delivery bird's name... I don't know who it's from—but whoever it is, they want a reply. I'll come back later to pick up your letter."

And off he swam at great speed.

Penguin began to read.

Dear You, Whoever You Are,
Who Lives on the Other Side
of the Horizon

I am Giraffe. I live in
Africa. I'm famous for my
long neck. Please tell me
all about yourself.

    Yours sincerely,

    Giraffe

Penguin had never heard of Giraffe. And he had never heard of a neck either.

"Professor, do you know Giraffe, who lives in Africa?"

"Let me see. I think I've heard the name before."

"Well then, do you know what a neck is? Giraffe says he has a long neck."

"Hmmm, isn't that the place under the head where it gets narrower?" The Professor did not seem too sure about this.

"Then where is your neck, Professor?"

"A brilliant question, Penguin! That'll be your next lesson."

In fact, the Professor did not know where his neck was either.

Penguin began examining the whale's enormous body from head to tail. After some time he suddenly shouted, "Aha! I've found it!"

Penguin patted the narrow spot just before the Professor's tail.

"Your neck must be here, sir, where it gets smaller. That means you have a VERY big head! In fact almost your whole body is head... Oh! Of course! That's why you're so smart!"

Penguin chattered away, very satisfied with his answer.

Although the Professor wasn't sure that this was quite right, he was pleased to be called smart.

"Bravo! An excellent answer!" he cried, and blew a great spout into the air. He listened for applause, but there was only silence. Looking around, he saw that Penguin was staring into the sea with a thoughtful expression.

"What are you doing?"

Penguin was gazing at his reflection in the water.

"Professor, where is *my* neck?"

But the Professor had no idea. "That'll be your homework for today," he announced. "School's out!"

The sea turned from blue to orange. But Penguin was no longer thinking about the blue mystery of the sea. His neck was a much more important problem.

He turned his back to the setting sun and stared at his long shadow stretching out in front of him.

Just then, Seal swam up. "Hello there, Penguin! Did you write a reply?"

"A reply? Oh, I forgot. I wonder what I should write." He must send something before the sun went down.

He wasn't quite sure what to say, but he wrote a letter anyway, and Seal rushed back to give it to Pelican.

"Sorry to keep you waiting. Here's your reply."
Seal showed him the letter.

But Pelican was busy eating.

"Mmmm. The fish here are pretty tasty…"
Only after gulping down the last fish did he take
the letter. Slowly, and a little clumsily, he flew
up into the sky.

He had eaten a bit too much.

I'd like to come back here again, he thought as he left Whale Sea behind.

By the time he reached the savanna and the impatient Giraffe, he was exhausted. Then he saw Giraffe's beaming face. *It may have been a hard trip*, he thought to himself, *but it was worth it.*

Penguin's Reply

Day came to the savanna, but Giraffe still did not read the letter. Even though he had been waiting so eagerly. Even though he had wished all night for morning to come.

"Not yet," he said to himself. "Not yet. Just a little longer."

It seemed such a waste to open the letter now.
He was so happy just to have it. He wanted to
relish that feeling for as long as he could.

Just then he heard a rustling sound. He
looked around, and there was Pelican, hiding in
the shadow of the leaves. Except that only his
head was hidden.

"Oh, it's you, Pelican. What are you doing here?"

"Oh, uh, nothing… Well, ahem, I was just wondering what the letter said."

Giraffe had forgotten that he wasn't the only one who was bored. Pelican was bored, too. It was time to read that letter.

"Pelican," he said. "I was just about to open it. Let's read it together."

"Really? I mean, I was thinking of taking the day off anyway, so if you want me to stay and read it with you, I could."

Actually Giraffe was Pelican's only customer so far, but he didn't say that.

When Giraffe finally opened the letter, his heart was pounding and his knees were trembling (and so were Pelican's).

Dear Giraffe,

I am penguin. I live at Whale Point.

When I read your letter, I learned for the first time that there is such a thing as a neck.

I think maybe I don't have a neck. Or maybe I am all neck?

Yours sincerely,
Penguin at Whale Point

Giraffe tilted his head to one side atop his own very long neck.

What on earth could Penguin mean? How could there be a body with no neck? Or a body that was all neck?

"Aha! That's it!" Pelican shouted. "His name is Penguin!" Not being able to remember the name had really been bugging him.

"Pelican," Giraffe said suddenly. "I know you were going to take the day off, but could you do that some other day? I want you to deliver another letter for me. I'll write it right now."

Pelican's eyes grew round. "You what?"

He was going to say, "No." After all, he had only come back yesterday from the other side of the horizon. But then he remembered all those tasty fish. And one other thing crossed his mind: the hardworking delivery seal.

The next thing he knew, he was saying, "Of course. Whale Point, right?"

Giraffe and Penguin Become Pen Pals

Even after sending his reply, Penguin could not stop thinking about Giraffe's letter. What on earth was a neck, and did he have one?

He was still wondering when Seal arrived with another letter from Giraffe.

Dear Penguin

Thank you for your letter.

I want to know more

about you. Please tell me.

For example, what do

you look like? And that

sort of thing.

Yours sincerely,

Giraffe

"What do I look like?" Penguin asked the Professor when they met for school that day.

"You're mostly black and white."

"That's what I thought," Penguin said.

Then he disappeared.

A moment later he returned with the bucket. Clankety-clank, clankety-clank.

And then he climbed inside.

"Professor," he asked, "am I *still* black and white?"

"Yes, you are the same. Black and white."

"Thank you, sir!" Penguin said with a big grin.

Dear Giraffe,

Thank you for your letter. You asked what I look like, but looking is a very odd thing.

At the moment I live on Whale Point, which is surrounded by sea, just like my home on Penguin Island. In the daytime, when the sun shines, the sea looks blue. But in the morning and the evening it looks completely different. And at night, it's different again.

And that's not all. No matter whether the sea looks blue or green or orange, when I scoop up a bucketful the water becomes transparent. Isn't that strange?

Perhaps it isn't looking that's strange, but the sea itself.

Or maybe it's the bucket.

But you asked what I look like. I think that I am mostly black and white. Even when I climbed into a bucket, my feathers did not change. So I think that must be right.

Yours sincerely,
Penguin at Whale Point

P.S. I think you and I would get along. I'm looking forward to your next letter.

Giraffe and Pelican read the letter together.

"Pelican," said Giraffe when they had finished, "I still wonder what on earth Penguin looks like."

"I could go and find out," Pelican suggested.

Whale Sea did not seem so far away now, and he wanted to see Whale Point. Pelican had never been there because Seal took care of delivering all the letters once they reached Whale Sea.

Giraffe looked tempted for a moment, but then he shook his head.

"No, don't do that. It's more fun imagining. I'm going to keep writing to Penguin and see if I can dress up to look like him. Will you help me?"

"You're going to try to look like Penguin? That's a crazy idea."

They both burst out laughing.

And that is how the once-bored Giraffe became pen pals with Penguin.

Dear Penguin,

It is so much fun trying to imagine what you look like when I have never met you. I am going to see if I can make myself a Penguin costume. And if it works, I want to come and meet you. So please tell me more about yourself.

Yours sincerely,

Giraffe Who Is Trying to Look Like You

On Whale Point, the Professor and Penguin had begun to look forward to Giraffe's letters, too.

"Professor! Giraffe says he wants to dress up to look like me!"

"You know, I've lived a long time," the Professor said, "but I've never heard of anything like this before." He perked up at the very thought of it.

Dear Giraffe Who Is Trying
to Look Like Penguin,

I'm very good at swimming
in the sea. I have a beak.
I use it to catch fish.

I can't wait to meet you.

Yours sincerely
Penguin at Whale Point

Dear Penguin,

My friend Pelican also has a beak. He loves fish too.

His name sounds like yours, so maybe he also looks like you.

Can you fly through the sky?

Yours sincerely,

Giraffe Who Is Trying to Look Like Penguin

Pelican was becoming a hard worker, just like Seal.

Of course, this was partly because the fish in Whale Sea were so delicious. But it was also because Pelican was having so much fun delivering Giraffe's letters.

He was also learning more about Seal. Seal's father, and his grandfather, and his grandfather's father, and the father of his grandfather's father, and the father of the father of his grandfather's father had all been in charge of the mail for Whale Sea. In fact, Seal was the tenth-generation delivery seal in his family.

"Wow! Ten generations!" Pelican exclaimed. "That's amazing!"

So once again, Pelican puffed up his chest,
flapped his wings, and flew towards the other
side of the horizon.

Dear Giraffe Who Is Trying
to Look Like Penguin,

I am afraid that I can't
fly through the sky.
I do have wings but they
are very small.

Yours sincerely,
Penguin at Whale Point

"He has wings but they're very small? Maybe they are just for decoration? What do you think, Pelican?"

Pelican was trying to figure out what Penguin looked like, too.

"Hmmm. He said he's good at swimming, right? But he can't fly. I wonder if he can walk."

Dear Penguin,

What do you do when you're
not swimming? Do you sit?
And can you walk? Pelican
wants to know.

Yours sincerely,

Giraffe

AFRICA

SOUTH POLE

Dear Giraffe,

When I'm not swimming
I stand up. I have two
legs, but they are very
short. I am quite good at
walking.

Yours sincerely,
Penguin at Whale Point.

"My goodness. He has two short legs, just like you, Pelican."

Their laughter drifted on the soft breeze. By this time, Pelican had begun to spend all his free time with Giraffe.

"Why don't we try drawing a picture of him?" he suggested.

"That's a great idea."

They read all of Penguin's letters over again.

Giraffe tilted his head. "Pelican, what do you think he means when he says he has no neck, or that maybe he is all neck?"

Just then a snake slithered by.

"Giraffe, look at that!" said Pelican. "You can't really tell if Snake has a neck or not, can you? He looks like he doesn't have one, but then again he looks like he is all neck. Maybe Penguin looks like him!"

"I bet you're right!" Giraffe said.

Giraffe drew a picture of a snake with a beak and two wings standing on two short legs.

"That looks very odd," he said.

"You look pretty odd yourself, now that I think about it," Pelican said.

He stared at Giraffe's long neck for some time. Then he said, "I bet Penguin means that he can't tell where his neck begins or ends. Like Snake."

Pelican drew a long straight body and added a beak, two wings and two legs.

"Oh, I see. Yes, that looks better... And he says he's black and white..."

They tried making the body black on one side and white on the other, then black on top and white on the bottom, and then added polka dots to see how that looked.

Just then, Zebra walked by.

"Giraffe, look!" Pelican said.

"Black and white!" they shouted.

And so their picture of 'Penguin' was done. *Now* Giraffe was ready to dress up like his pen pal.

Giraffe Dresses Up
Like Penguin

Dressing Giraffe up to look like the picture was going to be much harder than drawing it.

For starters, Penguin had only two legs, but Giraffe had four.

"Pelican, I've got two extra legs. What should I do?"

"Hmmm. That's going to be a problem all right," Pelican said. "Maybe we should cover your whole body with something. But I wonder what we could use…"

Pelican looked Giraffe up and down, then down and up.

"Wait a minute. I know! And I think I know where I can find some." And away he flew.

Find some what? Where? Giraffe wondered.

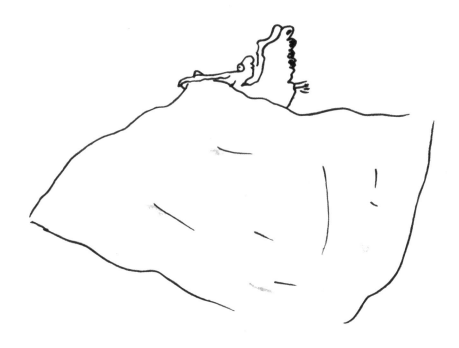

A little while later, Pelican returned carrying something white.

"What's that?" Giraffe asked, gazing up into the sky.

Pelican let the white thing fall. It spread open in the air and floated down onto the grass.

"It's cloth," Pelican said. "I thought this piece would be big enough to cover all of you. It looks just the right size." He wiped the sweat from his forehead.

"Where did you get it?"

"From Stork. It's for carrying babies. She was really busy as usual, but she said she never uses this one. Somehow I doubt she'll ever have to carry a baby this big, and she was happy to give it to us."

The soft cloth fit Giraffe perfectly. He sat wrapped up in it for some time, fondly thinking of his mother.

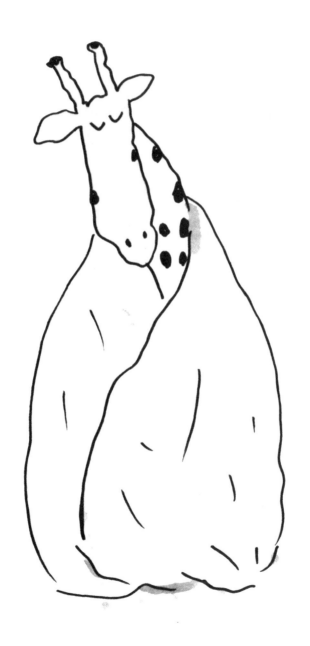

In the meantime, Pelican made a beak and feet just like his, and two little wings. Then he painted the cloth with black stripes just like Zebra's. Finally, he was finished.

"Hooray! We're done. Now you look *exactly* like Penguin!"

Dear Penguin,

We did it! Now I look just like you. So I'm coming to see you dressed up as you. I can hardly wait!

Yours sincerely,

Giraffe

As usual, Pelican delivered the letter special express.

Penguin was thrilled. He had invited his girlfriend, and his parents, and all his friends from his hometown to come. They were going to meet a giraffe for the very first time in their lives. And not just any old giraffe. They were going to meet a giraffe dressed up to look like Penguin.

They made a huge welcome banner.

"Giraffe Who Looks Like Penguin! Welcome to Whale Point!"

Everyone at Whale Point was busy getting ready to welcome Giraffe.

"This is so much fun!"

"I've never seen a giraffe before."

They were very excited.

Looking back over his long life, Professor Whale said, "Well, this was worth waiting for all these years."

Meanwhile, Giraffe and Pelican set off for Whale Point.

"The horizon is so far away."

"I told you so."

Giraffe was bursting with gratitude. "Thank you, Pelican."

"No, no, not at all. I should really thank you. Because you were once a bored giraffe, I'm no longer a bored pelican."

"And because we were bored, now we're friends."

"That's right. Which means that being bored is not all bad."

A warm, happy feeling filled their hearts.

At last, Whale Point came into sight!

Face to Face at Last

Any minute now, Pelican and Giraffe would arrive.

Everyone at Whale Point stared at the horizon, their hearts beating with excitement.

Something was coming…a raft pulled by Seal…with somebody on it. The closer it came, the more clearly they could see.

"Do you think that's him?" someone said.

"No, it can't be," another said. "I mean, he doesn't look like Penguin at all."

They had planned to welcome Giraffe with a great round of applause, but instead they stood frozen to the spot.

Penguin and Giraffe looked at each other. Their eyes met.

Giraffe had prepared a little speech, but now he could not say a word.

There was a long, awkward silence.

SWWWWHOOOOSH!!!

Suddenly, the Professor sent an extraordinarily magnificent spout into the air.

Everyone gasped, then they all began to clap and cheer at the spectacular display.

The applause got louder and louder, and soon they were all shouting, "Welcome Giraffe-who-looks-like-Penguin!"

Penguin dived into the sea and swam straight over to Giraffe, who did not look the least bit like Penguin. He jumped onto the raft and gave him a big hug.

"Thank you so much," he said. "I'm so happy to see you!"

Giraffe smiled, embarrassed. "I'm sorry. I don't look anything like you, do I?"

They looked at each other. Then they burst out laughing. And once they had started, they just could not stop. They'd never felt happier.

What Happened Next

What happened next, you ask?

Well, Giraffe-who-tried-to-look-like-Penguin
and Penguin-whom-Giraffe-tried-to-look-like
became the very best of friends. And, of course,
Penguin and Pelican did, too. Oh yes, and
Pelican and Seal as well.

As for Professor Whale, after that last
extraordinary spout, he found that he'd totally
run out of puff.

"Time for me to retire," he said. "There's nothing more to teach you, Penguin. You should go back home and become a teacher yourself."

Although Penguin was sad to say goodbye, he decided to do just what the Professor suggested. After all, it had always been his dream to go back to his island and build a school.

It was about time for him to get married, too, he
thought.

Seal and Pelican now work as a team,
delivering mail by sea and air. They're going to
be very busy delivering all the invitations for
Penguin's wedding.

Of course, Giraffe is no longer bored—but what
about the Professor? Now that he's retired,
won't he get bored, you ask?

Not at all! He's busy every day…writing
letters.

Dear You, Whoever You Are, Who
Lives on the other side of the Horizon.

I am Whale. I live at Whale Point.
My body is almost all head.
That's why I'm so smart, people say.

Please tell me all about yourself.

Yours sincerely,
    Whale at Whale Point.

Who knows? Maybe that very letter is on its way to your place right now.

From Whale at Whale Point

First American edition published 2017 by Gecko Press USA,
an imprint of Gecko Press Ltd

This edition first published in 2016 by Gecko Press
PO Box 9335, Marion Square, Wellington 6141, New Zealand
info@geckopress.com

Reprinted 2016

Boku wa Africa ni Sumu Kirin to Iimasu
Text © Megumi Iwasa 2001
Illustrations © Jun Takabatake 2001
First published in Japan in 2001 by KAISEI-SHA Publishing Co., Ltd, Tokyo
English translation rights arranged with KAISEI-SHA Publishing Co., Ltd
through Japan Foreign-Rights Centre

Distributed in the United States and Canada by
Lerner Publishing Group, www.lernerbooks.com
Distributed in the United Kingdom by
Bounce Sales and Marketing, www.bouncemarketing.co.uk
Distributed in Australia by Scholastic Australia, www.scholastic.com.au
Distributed in New Zealand by Upstart Distribution, www.upstartpress.co.nz

Translated by Cathy Hirano
Edited by Jolisa Gracewood
Design and typesetting by Katrina Duncan
Printed in China by Everbest Printing Co. Ltd,
an accredited ISO 14001 & FSC certified printer

Hardback (USA) ISBN: 978-1-927271-88-9
Paperback ISBN: 978-1-927271-87-2
Ebook available

For more curiously good books, visit www.geckopress.com